CAMILA
THE INVENTION STAR

written by ALICIA SALAZAR

illustrated by MÁRIO GUSHIKEN

cover artwork by THAIS DAMIÃO

PICTURE WINDOW BOOKS
a capstone imprint

Published by Picture Window Books, an imprint of Capstone
1710 Roe Crest Drive, North Mankato, Minnesota 56003
capstonepub.com

Library of Congress Cataloging-in-Publication Data
Names: Salazar, Alicia, 1973- author. | Gushiken, Mário, illustrator. | Damião, Thais, artist.
Title: Camila the invention star / written by Alicia Salazar ; illustrated by Mário Gushiken ; cover artwork by Thais Damião.
Description: North Mankato, Minnesota : Picture Window Books, an imprint of Capstone, [2023] | Series: Camila the star | Audience: Ages 5-7. | Audience: Grades K-1. | Summary: Inspired by her desire for late night snack, Camila invents a pair of light-up slippers, which make her a star to her classmates—but get her into trouble with her parents.
Identifiers: LCCN 2022041326 (print) | LCCN 2022041327 (ebook) | ISBN 9781484671030 (hardcover) | ISBN 9781484670996 (paperback) | ISBN 9781484671009 (pdf) | ISBN 9781484671061 (kindle edition)
Subjects: LCSH: Hispanic American girls—Juvenile fiction. | Inventions—Juvenile fiction. | Footwear—Juvenile fiction. | CYAC: Hispanic Americans—Fiction. | Inventions—Fiction. | Footwear—Fiction. | LCGFT: Picture books.
Classification: LCC PZ7.1.S2483 Cak 2023 (print) | LCC PZ7.1.S2483 (ebook) | DDC 813.6 [E]—dc23/eng/20220830
LC record available at https://lccn.loc.gov/2022041326
LC ebook record available at https://lccn.loc.gov/2022041327)

Designer: Hilary Wacholz

TABLE OF CONTENTS

Meet Camila and Her Family

Papá

Mamá

Ana, age 14

Andres, age 10

Camila, age 7

Spanish Glossary

ay, que susto (AI keh SOOS-toh)—ow, how scary

familia (fa-MEE-lee-ah)—family

gracias a Dios (GRAH-see-ahs ah DEE-ohs)—thank goodness or thank God

Mamá (mah-MAH)—Mom

mariposa (mah-ree-POH-sah)—butterfly

mija (MEE-ha)—my child

Papá (pah-PAH)—Dad

tía (TEE-ah)—aunt

Chapter 1
LATE NIGHT SNACK

Camila wanted a snack.
She looked at the clock next to
her bed. It was three o'clock in
the morning.

Camila's **familia** was sound asleep. "I will be quiet like a **mariposa**," she whispered to herself.

She tiptoed out of bed, put on her slippers, and opened her bedroom door.

In her room, the porch
light streamed in through
the windows. But there were
no windows in the hallway.
Everything was dark.

"I've walked down this hall a thousand times," Camila said. "I can do this."

Bump! Crash!

She walked right into a table and knocked a pair of metal candleholders onto the floor.

"¡Ay, que susto!" cried Camila.

Mamá and Papá and Ana and Andres came running out of their bedrooms.

"What was that?" asked
Andres.

"What are you doing?"
asked Ana.

"Are you hurt?" asked **Papá**.

"I just wanted a snack," said
Camila.

"At three in the morning?" said **Mamá**. "You have school tomorrow."

Camila shrugged her shoulders and picked up the candleholders.

"I'm sorry. I'll go back to bed," said Camila.

Chapter 2

A BRIGHT IDEA

Camila went back to her room, but she didn't go to sleep. She had a problem to solve.

She remembered the LED lights **Papá** had gotten her for her science project.

She took them out of the storage box in her closet. She carefully glued one LED light to the front of each of her slippers.

Camila waited until she was
sure everyone was asleep again.
Then she put on her slippers,
turned on the small lights, and
walked out of her room.

Camila could see with her light-up slippers. She didn't bump into anything.

She got all the way to the kitchen, opened the pantry, and quietly ate three fig cookies. No one woke up.

The next day at school Camila told her friends about her invention.

"What a great idea," said Bea.

"I need your invention," said Flor. "I always get hungry at night!"

"I have extra LED lights," said Camila. "Bring me your slippers, and I can put lights on them."

Chapter 3

PROBLEMS TO SOLVE

By the end of the week, all the kids in her class wanted LED slippers like Camila's. She was running out of LED lights!

Camila wrote out how to make the slippers and made copies. She shared the instructions with everyone who asked.

"You are an inventing star," said Bea.

Mamá picked Camila up from school "What's this about an invention?" she asked after Camila got buckled.

"What do you mean?" asked Camila, looking at Mamá sideways.

"Your **tía** called me to say she caught Flor getting a snack in the middle of the night," said **Mamá**. "She was wearing slippers with LED lights. It seems lots of kids in your school are using them."

"Am I in trouble?" asked Camila.

"There is nothing wrong with your invention," said **Mamá**. "But **Papá** and I want you to feel safe telling us what you are up to."

"I was afraid you would be mad that I was eating snacks in the middle of the night," said Camila.

"I know how many fig cookies there are in a package, Camila," said **Mamá**. "Everyone needs a snack sometimes. I'm not mad at you for that."

"**Gracias a Dios**," said Camila. "Because I am an inventing star now. I can't stop. There are so many more problems to solve."

"I can't wait to see what's next, **mija**," said **Mamá**.

Egg Drop!

Practice being an inventor with this classic activity: creating an egg drop container. Invite some friends to make their own containers. Then test them to see whose container works the best.

WHAT YOU NEED

- eggs
- small containers
- bubble wrap
- cotton balls
- tape
- ladder
- packing peanuts
- cardboard
- other materials of your choice. Use your imagination!

WHAT YOU DO

1. Each inventor can build the container they believe will best protect the egg. You may want to agree to limit the size of your container and add other rules as a group. Each inventor should end up with their egg secured in their container.

2. Once the eggs are secure, test the containers by dropping them from a few steps up on a ladder. Make sure each container is dropped from the same height.

3. Did your eggs survive? Make any repairs you might need and drop them from an even greater height. Whose container works the best?

Glossary

instructions (in-STRUHK-shuhns)—a set of actions to do to complete a task

invention (in-VEN-shuhn)—a new thing someone makes, often to solve a problem

LED (ELL EE DEE)—short for *light-emitting diode*, which is a device that makes light when electricity is sent through it. LED lights last a long time and do not break easily.

whisper (WIS-per)—to speak in a soft, breathy voice

Think About the Story

1. In the story, Camila woke up her whole family by sneaking into the hallway. Were you surprised when she snuck back out after saying she was going back to bed? What would you have done?

2. Camila's invention helped solve a problem. Think of a problem that you have or one a family member or friend has. Then think of an invention to solve the problem. Write a paragraph to explain what the problem is, what your invention is, and how it would solve the problem.

3. Can you think of other ideas that could have helped Camila with her nighttime snack problem?

About the Author

Alicia Salazar is a Mexican American children's book author who has written for blogs, magazines, and educational publishers. She was also once an elementary school teacher and a marine biologist. She currently lives in the suburbs of Houston, Texas, but is a city girl at heart. When Alicia is not dreaming up new adventures to experience, she is turning her adventures into stories for kids.

About the Illustrator

Mário Gushiken has been working as an illustrator since 2014. While he currently works mainly on book publishing projects, he has worked in the editorial, animation, advertising, and fashion industries. In his spare time, Mario likes to hang out with friends and play video games.